BUBBLE, THE FISH

NAVY-LOU, THE BIRD IN BLUE

HARVEY, THE MONKEY

PAT, THE CAT

MIA, THE MOUSE

RICK, THE CHICK

ROCKY, THE ROOSTER

HELEN, THE HEN

PIGGY, THE PIG

PEPE, THE PENGUIN

CHUCK, THE DUCK

ROGER, THE BADGER

TED, THE TOAD

OTTO, THE OCTOPUS

HERE IS THE STORY OF FOSSIL, A CROCODILE WHO CARRIES THE WEIGHT OF THE WORLD ON HIS SHOULDERS.
FROM FIPPO THE HIPPO TO OTTO THE OCTOPUS, A PARADE OF ANIMALS CLIMBS ON HIS BACK AND PUTS ON A REAL SHOW!
HOW EXCITING! ON EACH PAGE, TRY TO FIND, NAME, AND COUNT ALL OF FOSSIL'S FRIENDS!

WITH THE KIND HELP OF CHEWING GUM, THE SPARROW

Published by
Princeton Architectural Press
A McEvoy Group company
37 East 7th Street, New York, NY 10003
202 Warren Street, Hudson, NY 12534
Visit our website at www.papress.com

First published in France under the title
Tranquille comme Fossile
© 2014 hélium / Actes Sud, Paris, France

English edition
© 2017 Princeton Architectural Press
All rights reserved
Printed and bound in China
20 19 18 17 4 3 2 1 First edition

Editor: Nicola Brower

Special thanks to:
Janet Behning, Nolan Boomer, Abby Bussel,
Erin Cain, Tom Cho, Barbara Darko,
Benjamin English, Jenny Florence,
Jan Cigliano Hartman, Lia Hunt, Mia Johnson,
Valerie Kamen, Simone Kaplan-Senchak,
Jennifer Lippert, Sara McKay, Rob Shaeffer,
Sara Stemen, Paul Wagner, and Joseph Weston
of Princeton Architectural Press
—Kevin C. Lippert, publisher

Library of Congress
Cataloging-in-Publication Data
available upon request

THE QUIET CROCODILE

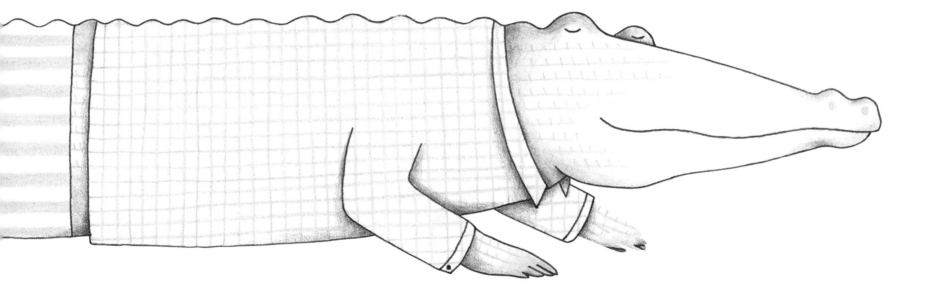

NATACHA ANDRIAMIRADO / DELPHINE RENON

PRINCETON ARCHITECTURAL PRESS · NEW YORK

FOSSIL, THE CROCODILE, LOVES THE QUIET.

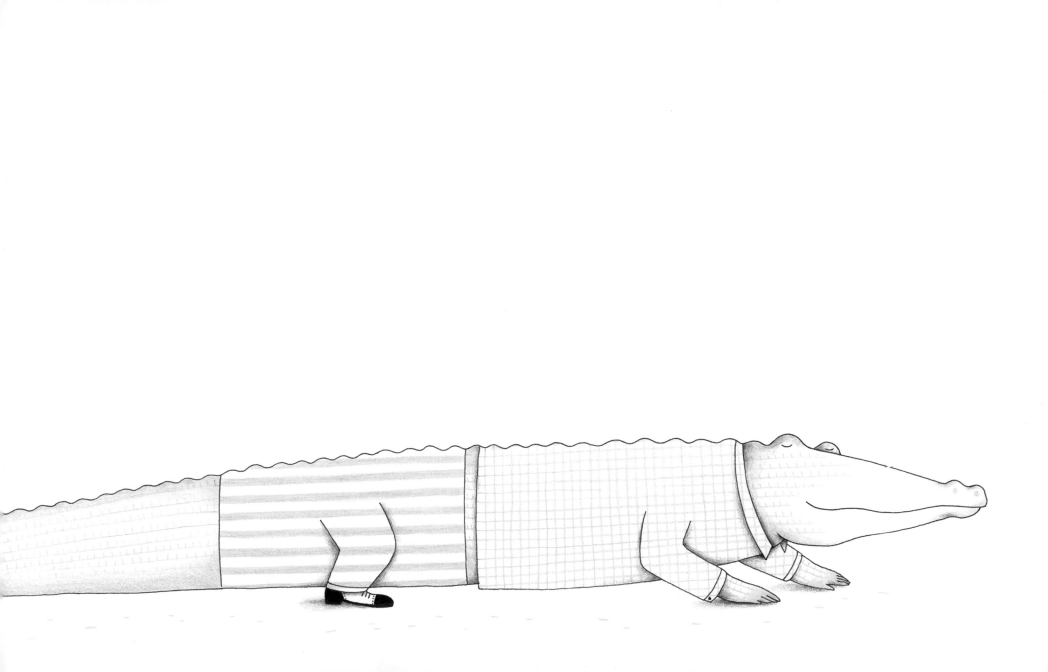

HIS FAVORITE THING IS TO DAYDREAM,
AND TO THINK.

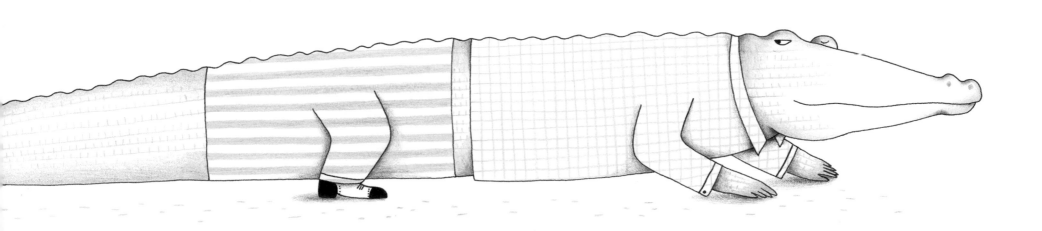

HE LIKES TO BE ALONE.

AWAY FROM ALL THE RACKET AND HUBBUB.

STILL, FOSSIL HAS A FEW FRIENDS.

HIS FRIENDS LOVE TO TALK.
EVEN IF HE IS A BIT QUIET.

THERE'S JUST ONE THING THAT BOTHERS FOSSIL.

HE'S AFRAID...

OF SCARING HIS FRIENDS.

OF COURSE!
CROCODILES ARE QUIET, BUT THEY ARE ALSO QUICK.
(AND, AS EVERYBODY KNOWS, THEY'RE FIERCE.)

EVEN IN BOOKS!

EVEN IN BOOKS?!

No, no, of course not!

HEY, FOSSIL!

come play with us!

FoooSsil!

FOSSIL!

OH... FOSSIllL!

FO-sSIL!

FoSSIL! FOSSIL! FOSSIL!

DON'T PLAY CROCODILE, FOSSIL!

FOSSIL IS A QUIET CROCODILE...

... AND QUICK!

FOSSIL, THE CROCODILE, LOVES THE QUIET.
HIS FAVORITE THING IS TO DAYDREAM, TO THINK,
AND TO BE...

WITH ALL HIS FRIENDS!

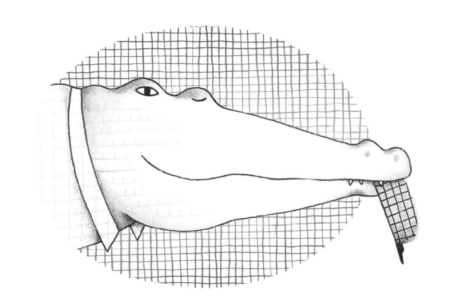

FIPPO, THE HIPPO

SONNY, THE BUNNY

RYAN, THE LION

MOOMOO, THE COW

SHERRY, THE SHEEP

ZOG, THE DOG

ZACHARY, THE ZEBRA

RUBYLETTE, THE BIRD IN RED

MYRTLE, THE TURTLE

TEDDY, THE BEAR